The Computer Munched My Homework and Other Classroom Jokes

by Dianne Woo

Illustrated by Jack White

TOR

A TOM DOHERTY ASSOCIATES BOOK
NEW YORK

First published 1992 as a Tor book by Tom Doherty Associates Inc., New York

First published in Great Britain 1994 by Pan Books Limited
a division of Pan Macmillan Publishers Limited
Cavaye Place London SW10 9PG
and Basingstoke

Associated companies throughout the world

ISBN 0 330 33975 3

9 8 7 6 5 4 3 2 1

A CIP catalogue record for this book is available from
the British Library

Printed and bound in Great Britain by
Cox & Wyman Ltd, Reading, Berkshire

Student: Teacher, may I leave the class?
Teacher: Well, you certainly can't take it with
    you.

*How do the cooks know there's enough bread
in the school cafeteria?*
    They take a roll call.

*What did the principal say when she got a call
from Mr. Hamm and a call from the mayor at
the same time?*
    "I'll have the Hamm, hold the mayor."

Billie: It hurts to hold my head up. I'd better go
    see the nurse.
Millie: Neck's weak?
Billie: No, I need to go right now!

What do you call the head of a fish school?
    The sar-dean. *(sardine)*

Why do oysters do so well in school?
    Because they have pearls of wisdom.

1

What do yuppie rabbits become after they finish business school?
Million-hares.

Teacher: Please help Cindy. She was playing the harmonica, and she swallowed it!
Nurse: I'm glad she wasn't playing the piano.

Student: Nurse, I feel like a deck of cards.
Nurse: Hold on, I'll deal with you later.

Teacher: Who can tell me what kind of animal
        life there is in Paris?
Joey: Rabbits. They're in the hutch—back of
        Notre Dame.

*Why did the band teacher hire tutors for her
students?*
   She thought they needed band-aids.

What's yellow and plays in the school orchestra?
   A band-ana.

Teacher: Class, who can tell me why Robin
        Hood and Maid Marian lived happily ever
        after?
Student: Because Robin heard what made
        marryin' great.

Maggie: Why are you carrying that rabbit's foot?
Mark: It's for good luck. I'm scared to death of
        tests.
Maggie: But we don't have a test today.
Mark: See! It's working!

3

What happened when the forgetful choir director found the door to his office locked?
He knew he needed to find the right key.

What's an ancient-history teacher's favorite TV show?
"Name That Tomb."

What's yellow outside, black and white inside, and very crowded?
A school bus full of zebras.

Did you hear about the soccer team that kept stumbling during their first game?
It was a real field trip.

Why is the head cook in the school cafeteria so mean?
Because he beats the eggs.

Coach: Did you do your exercises this morning?
Student: Yes, ma'am. I bent over and touched my shoes a hundred times.
Coach: Good! What did you do next?
Student: I took the shoes off the chair and put them on my feet.

What's a cheerleader's favorite flavor of ice cream?
    Rahs-berry.

Why did the chicken cross the playground?
    To get to the other slide.

Student: Nurse, I feel like a dog.
Nurse: Sit!

What's the difference between one classroom and two classrooms?
    Usually a wall.

How do you tell the difference between a person who is late for a train and a teacher in a girl's school?
    One misses the train, the other trains the misses.

When do 3 and 3 make more than 6?
    When they make 33.

Mother: How were the crackers in your lunch today, Jimmy?
Jimmy: Crummy.

What song do custodians like best?
  "Singin' in the Drain."

What never went to school but can speak every language?
  An echo.

Lizzie: I forgot everything I learned in school
    today.
Mother: Well, what do you know?

*What did the home economics teacher say
when he dropped an egg on his foot?*
  "The yolk's on me."

Teacher: Why were the Middle Ages called the
      Dark Ages?
Casey: Because there were so many knights.

How can three ones equal two?
  $1 + \frac{1}{1} = 2$.

How many times can you subtract 2 from 10?
  Just one time, because after you subtract it
  once, you no longer have 10.

Teacher: Class, who can tell me what country
      needs the most food?
Student: Hungary.

What's the difference between 10 and 100?
  Zero. (0)

Teacher: Class, what country is popular on
      Thanksgiving Day?
Student: Turkey.

Where did the cooking teacher go on vacation?
  Greece. *(grease)*

Teacher: What did Paul Revere say when he
      finished his famous ride?
Zoey: "Whoa!"

Why are the best students always on the run?
  Because they are pursuing their studies.

Tim: "Tammy taught the tiny tots to talk." How
      many T's are there in that?
Mike: There are only two T's in "that."

What vowel makes the most noise?
  An O, because all the other vowels are in-
  audible. *(in the word "audible")*

What kind of test does a spelling teacher give?
  N–X–M.

Kerry: My sister is really smart. She can spell her
      name backwards, and she's only in the first
      grade.
Harry: That's great! What's her name?
Kerry: Hannah.

Cal: The brain is a wonderful invention, but I can't figure it out.

Hal: What makes you say that?

Cal: Well, it starts working the minute you get up in the morning and never stops until the moment the teacher calls on you in class.

What two siblings were never wrong?
    The Wright Brothers.

Teacher: If you worked for ten hours at a wage
of one dollar per hour what would you get?
Student: A new job.

*What do the classroom, the playground, and
baseball have in common?*
They all have slides.

Father: Did you take an art class today?
Son: No, why? Is there one missing?

Teacher: Sally, what is 6 plus 7?
Sally: I don't know, I only have 10 fingers.

What did the acorn say when she grew up?
"Gee-om-a-tree!" *(Geometry)*

What kind of cars do government officials drive?
Civics.

Where does Rambo work out?
On the jungle gym.

Why did Suzy jog while studying for her test?
She wanted to get a physical education.

What do you say to your spelling teacher when she slips on the ice?
  R–U–O–K?

Teacher: If a Russian ruler is called a czar, and his wife is called a czarina, what are his children called?
Student: Czardines?

What do Santa's children carry in their lunch boxes?
  Ho-Ho's.

Ellen: Hey, I found 50 cents in front of school today!

Helen: Oh, that's mine. I dropped a half-dollar there this morning.

Ellen: But I found two quarters!

Helen: Well, it probably broke when it hit the pavement.

What piece of playground equipment taught the girl after school?
   Tutor-totter. *(Tutor taught her)*

What did the pencil say to the eraser?
   Nothing. Pencils can't talk.

How can you get a female dog to do new tricks?
   Teacher. *(teach her)*

What happens when kids go to school year-round?
   Some aren't on vacation and summer. *(some are)*

What did the eye doctor say to the teacher?
   "Your pupils need classes."

12

Teacher: How well do you like art?
Student: I don't know, I've never even met him.

What's a music teacher's favorite animal?
  A horned toad.

What did the spelling teacher say to the gorilla?
  U–R–N–N–M–L.

Teacher: Who can tell me what Camelot was
      famous for?
Sam: Its knight-life!

What's a geography teacher's favorite food?
  Eskimo pies.

What food do gym teachers like best?
  Bar-bell-cue ribs.

Principal: Well, young man, this is the fifth
      straight day you've been late to class. Have
      you anything to say for yourself?
Student: Boy, am I glad it's Friday!

13

Where's a gym teacher's favorite place to visit?
  The Golf of Mexico.

What's a gym teacher's favorite TV show?
  "Star Track."

What food do music teachers like best?
  Drumsticks.

What did the spelling teacher say after a long, hard day?
  I–M–C–P.

Why is riding a bike over barbed wire like a music lesson?
  You get sharps and flats.

Larry: Psst! How long did the War of 1812 last?
Mary: One year, then it became the War of
      1813.

What do you say when your library book is overdue?
  "Fine!"

What kind of sandwich gets all the attention in the cafeteria?
    A ham sandwich.

What's green and white, and scared when you open your lunch box?
    A chicken salad sandwich.

What snack is like the school bell?
    Ding Dongs.

Jenny: My sandwich is bigger than your salami
     sandwich.
Benny: That's baloney!
Jenny: You're right.

What did the bread say to the muffin?
    "Meet me behind the school cafeteria and
    we'll e-loaf." *(elope)*

*What do you get when you cross a building of
education with a boxer who's been knocked
out?*
    School daze.

What did the pencil say to the eraser?
    "Get the lead out."

Willy: Teacher, I know a company in Asia which
    makes writing liquid.
Teacher: Oh, yes? What is it called?
Willy: India, Inc. *(ink)*

*What happened when the computer was late to
the school cafeteria?*
    He couldn't get a byte.

What did the ruler say to the compass when they got into a fight?
   "I get the point! Let it slide!"

What's a wood-shop teacher's favorite food?
   Chipped beef.

What's a wood-shop teacher's favorite science-fiction film?
   "Saw Wars."

Father: I heard you played hooky from school today and played baseball with your friends.
Son: No, Dad, and I have the fish to prove it!

Why did the computer and the disk fight over the car?
   Because the computer wouldn't let the disk drive.

Math teacher: Henry, how many feet are in a yard?
Henry: Depends how many people are in it.

17

Why did the music teacher get glasses?
  So he could C-sharp.

Librarian: Shh! Can't you kids see the sign? It
      says "Silence!"
Student: We were just giving each other some
      sound advice.

*What did the eraser do when she fought with
the pencil?*
  She rubbed him out.

*Why did the drama student leap forward when
she saw another student actor tumble off the
stage?*
  She wanted to catch a falling star.

Todd: I tell the best riddles in school!
Rod: You must be joke-King. *(joking)*

What is a fruit's favorite subject?
  Currant events.

How do you make a slide rule?
  Give him a crown, a robe, and a scepter.

When is a school bus not a school bus?
    When it turns into a parking lot.

Nurse: Let me take your temperature.
Student: No way! It's the only one I've got!

Did you hear the joke about the broken pencil?
    There's no point to it.

Bill: My teacher must really like me.
Gil: What makes you say that?
Bill: She's kept me in her class four years in a
    row.

What's a baseball coach's motto?
    "If at first you don't succeed, try for second."

Tammy: Our class has to sing all of "America
    the Beautiful" every single day! It takes too
    much time.
Sammy: You're lucky. We have to sing the
    "Stars and Stripes" forever!

What's black and white and red all over?
    A textbook.

19

Teacher: Who was the Englishman who built up the British navy?
Student: Sir Launch-a-lot.

What do you call the study of famous women?
  Herstory.

Bertha: Somebody stole all the pastries out of the cafeteria!
Bella: Well, doesn't that take the cake!

What's the difference between a dog with fleas and a bored student?
  One is going to itch, the other is itching to go.

What's the difference between an obedient dog and a disobedient student?
  One rarely bites, the other barely writes.

John: Teacher, I know who built the first airplane that *didn't* fly.
Teacher: Who was that?
John: The Wrong Brothers.

What's the first thing an ape learns in school?
  The Ape–B–C's.

20

Why did the letter E flunk?
  It was always in bed and never in school.

Chemistry teacher: Who can tell me the formula
    for water?
Student: H, I, J, K, L, M, N, O.
Teacher: That's not correct.
Student: I thought you said that formula was H
    to O.

21

A mother was talking to the school psychologist about her son. "I'm worried about him. He thinks he's a monkey. All day long he swings from trees."

The psychologist told her, "Don't worry, ma'am. I'm sure it's just a phase. He'll grow out of it."

The mother looked relieved. "Oh, thank you, doctor. How much do I owe you?"

"Forty bananas," the doctor replied.

Teacher: What do you get when you divide 327,910 by 3?
Student: The wrong answer.

How did the astronaut's daughter pack her food?
In a launch box.

What do you do when your computer wants a snack?
Feed it microchips.

What do music teachers drink when they're thirsty?
Root-beer flutes.

What does a class of monkeys sing?
  "The Star-Spangled Banana."

What seafood do gym coaches like best?
  Mussels. *(muscles)*

History teacher: Class, did you know John Paul
    Jones was famous for saying, "I have not
    yet begun to fight!"?
Student: No wonder his side lost!

How is a bad riddle like an unsharpened pencil?
  It has no point.

An absent-minded principal arrived home in
the evening after working late at school. When
he got to the door of his house, he realized he
had forgotten his key. He knocked on the door.
  His wife looked out the peephole, but it was
so dark that she didn't recognize him. "I'm
sorry, sir," she said, "but my husband isn't
home yet."
  The absent-minded principal thought a
moment, then said, "All right, I'll come back
tomorrow."

Teacher: What are you painting, Mary?
Mary: It's a picture of a cow eating grass.
Teacher: Where is the grass?
Mary: The cow ate it.
Teacher: But where is the cow?
Mary: Well, why would he hang around if all the grass is gone?

What has stripes and sits at the head of the class?
The flag.

Teacher: I can hardly read your handwriting. You must try to write more clearly.
Timmy: If I did that, then you'd complain about my spelling.

Where can a student find money easily?
In the dictionary.

Why can't elephants go to college?
Because most can't graduate from high school.

Who wrote the Bad Student's Handbook?
I. M. Lazee.

Barb: Teacher, I think there's a rabbit in my computer.

Teacher: Good heavens! What makes you say that?

Barb: I keep getting floppy disks.

What do you call a teacher who shouts?
  A loud speaker.

Candy: On our field trip to the farm we saw a hen that laid an egg five inches long. Can you beat that?

Sandy: Yes, with an eggbeater.

Millie: When I grow up, I want to be a vitamin.
Jillie: Don't be silly. You can't be a vitamin.
Millie: Yes, I can. I saw a sign in a store window
that said "Vitamin B-1."

What resembles half of a basketball?
The other half.

Teacher: What is the hardest thing for you in
school?
Student: Whispering to my friend without
moving my lips.

Why couldn't Joey take tennis lessons after
school?
His mother didn't want him to raise a racket.

Principal: Did you see which way the computer
went?
Student: Data way! *(that a way)*

Teacher: Did you think the test questions were
hard?
Student: No, the questions were easy. It was the
answers that were hard.

What subject do cows like best?
   Moo-sic.

Student: I wish I had been born a hundred
      years ago.
History teacher: Why?
Student: Because I'd have one hundred less
      years of history to study.

Geography teacher: Where are the Great
      Plains?
Student: At the airport.

Why do birds hang around libraries?
   To catch bookworms.

Teacher: What is the most important thing to
      remember in chemistry class?
Student: Don't lick the spoon.

What subject do bees like best?
   Buzz-ness. *(business)*

English teacher: What is an autobiography?
Student: A book about a car's life.

What does your spelling teacher get when she rides the merry-go-round too many times?
   D–Z.

Geography teacher: Where can we find fjords?
Student: In the parking lot.

What do you get when you cross a math teacher with a crab?
   Snappy answers.

Teacher: Why will TV never replace the
   newspaper?
Student: You can't swat flies with a TV.

What do you call the back door of the cafeteria?
   The bacteria.

Driving instructor: Why isn't it a good idea to
   use snow tires in the summer?
Student: They might melt.

If there is a head of the class and a bottom of the class, what's in between?
   The student body.

Student: I didn't deserve a zero on this paper!
Teacher: I know, but it was the lowest grade I
could give you.

Principal: Are you trying to tell me that your
teacher yelled at you for something you
didn't do?
Student: Yes, my homework.

Why are fish so smart?
They hang out in schools.

Mother: Your teacher said you're at the bottom of your class.

Student: That's OK, we learn the same at both ends.

Which insect is the smartest?
  The spelling bee.

Science teacher: Which bird is smarter, the owl or the chicken?

Student: The owl.

Teacher: How do we know?

Student: Have you ever eaten Kentucky Fried Owl?

Why is one foot greater than three feet?
  One foot makes a ruler.

Geography teacher: Open your books to page 14. Who can tell me where Rome is?

Student: On page 15.

Student: I'll be home sick tomorrow.

Teacher: I didn't know you were feeling ill.

Student: I'm not now, but I will be after my dad sees my report card.

What do you feed a hungry cheerleading squad?
   Cheer-ios!

Why do math teachers dice their carrots?
   They like square roots.

What did the tall teacher say to the short student?
   "Speak up when you talk to me."

Student: I'm not going to Spanish class today.
Teacher: Why not?
Student: My throat hurts and I can barely speak
      English.

What's a teacher's favorite nation?
   Expla-nation.

Teacher: I hope I didn't see you looking at your
      neighbor's paper.
Student: I hope you didn't either.

Gym teacher: What's the hardest thing about
      learning to walk the balance beam?
Student: The gym floor.

31

What's a science teacher's favorite TV show?
   "Whale of Fortune."

Father: Do you have anything positive to say
      about my son?
Teacher: Yes, with grades like these he certainly
      can't be cheating.

*What did the track coach say after a long, hard
day?*
   "I can't wait to run a bath."

Dance instructor: There are two things that can
      keep anyone from being a good dancer.
      Do you know what they are?
Student: Yes, one's feet.

What's a music teacher's favorite food?
   Minuet rice.

Mother: How do you like your new school?
Student: Closed!

What word is very smart, yet dumb?
   Wis-dumb. *(wisdom)*

Teacher: Where is Moscow located?
Student: In the barn with Pa's cow.

What's in the middle of every class?
  The letter A.

What letter is not found in the alphabet?
  The kind you mail.

Science teacher: How can we get the mercury
    to go up and down?
Student: Put it in an elevator.

*When is a classroom like two letters of the
alphabet?*
    When it is M–T. *(empty)*

Principal: I thought I told you never to walk into
    school late again!
Student: I know, that's why I'm running.

*Why shouldn't a Chinese-food chef play pitcher
in a baseball game?*
    Because he woks everyone.

Teacher: I'd like to go one day without giving
    you detention!
Student: OK, how about today?

What plays hangman and flies?
    A spelling bee.

Why are textbooks and tall buildings alike?
    They both contain many stories.

Music teacher: What's an operetta?
Student: Someone who works for the phone
company.

*What word is usually pronounced wrong by
teachers?*
Wrong.

History teacher: Which leader do you think
made the biggest mistake in history?
Student: Noah. He should have swatted both
flies when he had a chance.

Teacher: I don't want you talking in class
anymore!
Student: That's OK. I don't need to talk any
more, I'm talking enough already.

Music teacher: Why are you banging the side of
your head on the piano?
Student: I'm playing by ear.

Math teacher: If I had five cows and ten goats,
what would I have?
Student: Plenty of milk.

What's furry, barks, and loves school?
  A teacher's pet.

Student: Mom, will you do my homework?
Mother: No, it wouldn't be right.
Student: That's OK, as long as you just do your
      best.

What question must a student always answer
with "yes"?
  "What does Y–E–S spell?"

History teacher: What do George Washington and Abraham Lincoln have in common?
Student: They're both dead.

How can eight 8's be added to make 1,000?
  $888 + 88 + 8 + 8 + 8 = 1,000.$

First student: A, B, C, D, E, F, G. What comes next?
Second student: Whiz!

What do you call two students coming on campus after hours?
  A pair of sneakers.

Teacher: Where was Queen Elizabeth crowned?
Student: On her head.

Where do carpenters study?
  Boarding school.

Principal: Your teacher said that you missed school yesterday.
Student: No, I was so busy fishing, I didn't miss school at all!

Why are eye doctors good teachers?
   They know how to treat pupils.

Geography teacher: What is the first thing you
      think of when I say Greece?
Student: My bicycle chain!

History teacher: Where was the Declaration of
      Independence signed?
Student: At the bottom.

*Why did the teacher prefer to have 30 students
instead of 20?*
   He wanted to have more class.

Teacher: Why does Billy run all the way home
      every day after school?
Student: He's trying to break Babe Ruth's
      consecutive home-run record.

Teacher: Are you having trouble hearing?
Student: No, I'm having trouble listening.

Which teacher wears the largest hat?
   The one with the largest head.

What's a witch's favorite subject?
Spelling.

What was the computer's medical diagnosis?
  Terminal.

Teacher: Which month has 28 days?
Student: All of them do.

Which is easier to spell, "eat" or "feed"?
  "Feed" is spelled with more ease. *(E's)*

School counselor: I would suggest you enroll in
      night school.
Student: Oh no, I couldn't do that! I can't read
      in the dark.

*Why did the student bring a pair of scissors to
school?*
  She wanted to cut class.

Student: Mom, I can't take any more baths.
Mother: Why not?
Student: My teacher said that if I get into hot
      water again, I'll be expelled.

Can pencils start anything?
  No, they can only be lead.

Mother: My son said that he got 100 on all his tests.

Teacher: He did—25 in spelling, 25 in math, 25 in history, and 25 in science.

Why do soccer players get the best grades?
Because they use their heads.

Teacher: Here's your report card.

Student: I don't want to scare you, but my dad said that if this report card is bad, the person responsible is going to be spanked!

What do you call a computer that hasn't been used for a long time?
Key-bored. *(keyboard)*

Teacher: This is the fifth time this week you've been late. What do you think I should do about it?

Student: Don't wait.

Student: I think my teacher is dumb.

Father: Why do you think that?

Student: He's always asking the class questions.

41

Teacher: How did people entertain themselves
in the Middle Ages?
Student: They went to knight-clubs.

Where does a track star wash her shoes?
Under running water.

Teacher: Do you know what this "F" on your
    homework means?
Student: "Fantastic"?

Father: What did you learn in school today?
Student: Writing.
Father: What did you write?
Student: I don't know, we haven't learned to
    read yet.

Student: I'm having a hard time learning how to
    spell.
Teacher: Why?
Student: Because all the words are different.

Teacher: Did you throw this rock through my
    classroom window?
Student: Yes, but it wasn't my fault.
Teacher: Whose fault was it?
Student: Johnny's—he ducked.

Math teacher: If I gave you one dollar each
    week for a whole year, what would you
    have?
Student: A new bike.

Teacher: Why is your essay about your pet exactly the same as your sister's?
Student: We have the same pet.

Teacher: Did your mother help you with your homework?
Student: No, she did it all by herself.

Teacher: Can you give me Lincoln's Gettysburg Address?
Student: I thought he lived in the White House.

Teacher: Why did you get such a low score on today's test?
Student: The girl who sits next to me is absent.

Teacher: The test time is almost up. How far are you from getting the correct answers?
Student: Two desks away.

What's the difference between a teacher and a train engineer?
   A teacher trains minds, an engineer minds trains.

Student: My new school is haunted.
Mother: How do you know?
Student: My teacher is always talking about
    school spirit.

45

Bus driver: Do you want to go to the junior high school or the senior high school?
Student: Neither, but I have to.

Student: I ain't got a pencil.
Teacher: I *haven't* got a pencil.
Student: That makes two of us.

Teacher: What do you think you'll be when you get out of school?
Student: Old!

Band director: Do you know how to clean your tuba?
Student: With a tuba toothpaste?

Math teacher: What's the difference between 2 and 5?
Student: The five is upside-down.

Student: My teacher can't make up her mind.
Mother: What do you mean?
Student: First she says that 2 and 2 is 4, and then she says that 3 and 1 are 4!

*How would you feel if you were kept after
school for failing the spelling test?*
   Spellbound.

Teacher: Can anyone tell me one thing that
      cowhide is used for?
Student: To hold the cow together.

Teacher: Did you study for this exam?
Student: Yes, I spent 8 hours on my book last
      night.
Teacher: Really?
Student: Yes, I fell asleep studying and slept on
      it all night.

Teacher: Do you know what the center of
      gravity is?
Student: "V."

What food do drama teachers like best?
   Ham.

Teacher: What is the plural of child?
Student: Twins.

What do spelling teachers eat for lunch?
  Alphabet soup.

Keith: How many sheep does it take to make one wool sweater?
Kathy: Gee, I didn't even know sheep could knit.

Teacher: If you study hard, you'll get ahead.
Student: No thanks, I already have a head.

Principal: Why are you running down the hall with that book in your hands?
Student: I'm speed-reading.

What is a snake's favorite subject?
  Hiss-tory.

Mother: Why did you get a zero on this homework assignment?
Student: That's not a zero. The teacher ran out of stars so she gave me a moon.

Teacher: Where is the English channel?
Student: I don't know, we don't get cable.

Lonnie: When I grow up, I want to be an Olympic athlete and a brilliant computer scientist.
Ronnie: Really? At the same time?
Lonnie: Yes, I'll be a floppy-discus thrower.

Grandmother: Do you like going to school?
Student: Yes, I like going and coming, but not the in-between part.

Student: I don't like history class.
Mother: Why not?
Student: Because my teacher keeps asking me about things that happened before I was born!

49

Teacher: I'm going to have to write a letter to your parents about this poor essay.
Student: I wouldn't do that.
Teacher: Why not?
Student: They wrote it.

How does a math teacher fix a leaky faucet?
With multi-pliers.

Why are history teachers never lonely?
They know a lot of dates.

Teacher: If I lay two eggs here, and three eggs here, how many eggs will there be?
Student: None. I don't believe you can lay eggs.

If a fish took a foreign language class, what would it be?
Finn-ish.

Teacher: How do we know that George Washington was a general and not an admiral?
Student: An admiral would have known better than to stand up in a boat.

Why did the vampire take a typing course?
   He wanted to learn different blood types.

Why do you have to buy school supplies every year?
   Because you can't get them for free.

Teacher: Name one animal that we get fur from.
Student: Skunks.
Teacher: Are you sure?
Student: Yup! My daddy says that if I see a
skunk I "shud git as fur from it" as I kin!

Where did Sir Lancelot get his education?
Knight school.

Student: I'm going to be an astronaut and fly to
the sun.
Teacher: You can't fly to the sun—it's too hot.
Student: Then I'll go at night.

First child: Want to play school?
Second child: Only if I can be absent.

History teacher: Who said, "Give me liberty or
give me death?"
Student: Someone in detention.

Why did the rabbit get an "A" in math?
She was good at multiplication.

How do you spell jealousy?
I–N–V–U.

Astronomy teacher: What do we call a star with a tail?
Student: Mickey Mouse.

Teacher: Can you define ignorance?
Student: I don't know what that means.
Teacher: That's correct.

Teacher: If you put your hand in your pocket and found 2 quarters, 6 nickels, and a dime, what would you have?
Student: Someone else's pants on!

Shop teacher: You hammer nails like lightning.
Student: You mean I'm very fast?
Shop teacher: No, you never strike twice in the same place.

Teacher: Any 8-year-old should be able to do these math problems.
Mother: Oh, well, no wonder my son can't do them. He's 12.

Father: What kind of marks are you getting in gym class?
Student: Bruises.

How do you make children grow?
  Put them in a kinder-garden.

What piece of furniture is good at math?
  A multiplication table.

First student: Do you believe in telling the future in cards?

Second student: Yes, I can take one look at my report card and know what my father will do when I get home.

How do you spell conceited?
  I—M—B—4—U.

How do bees get to school?
  They take a school buzz. *(bus)*

Teacher: I'm going to have to ask your mother to visit me.

Student: You'll be sorry.

Teacher: Why?

Student: My mother is a doctor and she charges $100 for a visit.

What word contains 26 letters but has only three syllables?
  Alphabet.

What teacher is always getting things wrong?
  Miss Take. *(mistake)*

Teacher: What do you get when you cut a
tomato into two parts?
Student: Halves.
Teacher: Into four parts?
Student: Quarters.
Teacher: What do you get when you cut the
quarters in half?
Student: Eighths.
Teacher: And what do you get when you cut
the eighths in half?
Student: Diced tomatoes.

Why are math teachers always sad?
They have so many problems.

Mother: What did your teacher say when you
told her you were an only child?
Student: She said, "Thank goodness!"

Why is cabbage the smartest vegetable?
It has a head.

Teacher: Today we're going to talk about the
shape that our world is in.
Student: We already know that it's round!

Where did the skating teacher go on vacation?
  Iceland.

Why do owls do well in school?
  They give a hoot!

Teacher: Has anyone ever heard the term
    "financial genius"?
Student: Yes, my mother said that it is someone
    who can make money faster than I spend
    it.

How do you spell flirtatious?
  U–R–A–Q–T.

Teacher: Why are you running?
Student: I'm running to stop a fight.
Teacher: Who is fighting?
Student: Me and the guy chasing me.

First student: Would you be scared if you saw a
    man-eating lion?
Second student: No.
First student: Why not?
Second student: I'm a girl!

What happens to bad eggs at school?
  They get eggs-spelled. *(expelled)*

Teacher: Why did you keep pulling your tongue out of your mouth during the test?
Student: The answers were on the tip of my tongue.

Mother: What did you learn about in math class today?
Student: A couple of trees.
Mother: Trees?
Student: Yes, gee-om-uh-tree and trig-o-nom-uh-tree.

Why don't math teachers fear crime?
There's safety in numbers.

Teacher: Why did you push your bike all the way to school today?
Student: I was so late I didn't have time to get on it.

Why is arithmetic tiring?
You have to carry so many numbers.

What did the teacher say to the clock?
"Quit tocking in my class!"

Why did the music teacher bring ladders to class?
He wanted his students to sing higher.

60

How do computers eat?
  In megabytes.

What does a skeleton do before a big exam?
  He bones up on things.

Teacher: You have 10 fingers. If you had four
    less, what would you have?
Student: No more piano lessons!

Why did the biology student get expelled?
  He got caught counting his ribs during an
  exam.

Teacher: Robert Burns wrote "To a Field
    Mouse."
Student: I bet the mouse never replied!

Teacher: If I had four oranges in this hand and
    ten apples in this hand, what would I have?
Student: Big hands!

*What do you get when you cross a dog with a
piano teacher?*
  A dog whose Bach is worse than its bite.

61

School nurse: You look tired.
Student: I am. I was up all night studying for my
blood test.

Mother: How do you know my son was
cheating?
Teacher: His answers are exactly the same as
the boy who sits next to him, except for
one.
Mother: Well, if that one answer is different, isn't
it possible that this is just a coincidence?
Teacher: I don't think so. The other boy's
answer was, "I don't know." Your son's
answer was, "Me neither."

Teacher: *(to calm down the class)* Order, please!
Student: I'll have a root-beer float.

Student: Can you write in the dark?
Father: I think so.
Student: Good, close your eyes and sign my
report card.

How do you spell sneeze?
   H–U!

What TV show do custodians like best?
   The soaps.

Why are students' grades lower after Christmas break?
   Because things always get marked down after Christmas.

Teacher: If Shakespeare was alive today, would he be considered famous?
Student: I hope so, he'd be the only person ever to live more than 400 years!

63

Student: I'm glad I wasn't born in France.
French teacher: Why?
Student: Because I can't speak French.

Grammar teacher: Can anyone tell me why
    punctuation is so important?
Student: Yes, if you're not punctual, you get
    detention.

Teacher: What three words are used regularly
    by high school students?
Student: I don't know.
Teacher: That is correct.

How do you spell spying?
    I–C–U.

Teacher: Why are you late?
Student: I was late when I left home.
Teacher: Why didn't you leave home earlier?
Student: Because it was too late to leave earlier.

History teacher: What was one benefit of the
    invention of the automobile?
Student: It reduced horse-stealing.

64

Father: Your teacher says you need to learn to write more clearly.

Student: I know how to write clearly, but I don't want to.

Father: Why not?

Student: If I wrote clearly, my teacher would know that I can't spell.

Teacher: An elephant never forgets.

Student: What do they have to remember?

School nurse: Cover your right eye and read the last line of the chart.

Student: It's spelled E–P–Y–H–L–N–O–Q, but I can't pronounce it.

Mother: How could you have received a "D" in conduct and an "A" in courtesy?

Student: Every time I hit someone I apologize.

Substitute teacher: What is your name?

Kindergartner: Mikey.

Substitute teacher: Mikey what?

Kindergartner: Um . . . Mikey, please pay attention?

Math teacher: Today we're going to study the formula "Pi r-squared."

Student: That's silly. Everyone knows that pies are round!

How do you spell skyscraper?
   N–D–C–T.

Why did the student purposely fail his history test?
   He wanted to go down in history.

Student driver: Why did you fail me on my driving test?

Driving instructor: Don't you realize that you barely missed that pedestrian?

Student driver: Well, if you give me a second chance, I'm sure I can hit her this time.

Teacher: What is the longest word in the English language?

Student: Smiles.

Teacher: That's only six letters.

Student: Yeah, but there is a whole mile between the first letter and the last.

Principal: Did you bring that note home to your parents?

Student: No sir. I lost it in a fight with another kid who said you weren't the best principal in the world.

Teacher: When I was your age, I could name all of the states in alphabetical order.

Student: Yeah, but there were a lot less states when you were my age.

Student: Do you think that it's fair to punish someone for something they didn't do?

Father: Of course not.

Student: Good, because I didn't do well on my exam.

Mother: Would you like a hand with your homework tonight, Son?

Student: No thanks, Mom, I'll get it wrong all by myself this time.

Teacher: Does anyone know Washington's farewell address?

Student: Wasn't he living in Virginia?

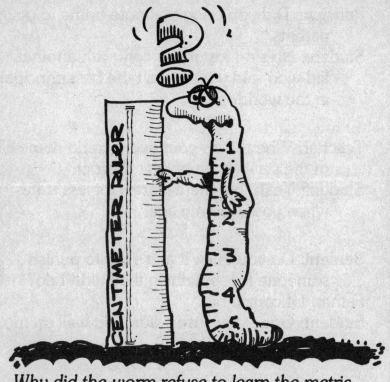

Why did the worm refuse to learn the metric system?

It was an inchworm.

Music teacher: It's amazing to think that
instruments such as the electric guitar had
their beginnings over 2,000 years ago.
Student: That's impossible, they didn't even
have electricity back then!

Teacher: How can you tell a weed from a good plant?
Student: Pull everything out of the garden and the things that grow back are weeds.

Student: Did you know that the longest sentence only contains three words?
Teacher: Oh, really? Give us an example.
Student: Life in prison.

Student: I'm related to George Washington.
Teacher: Are you sure?
Student: Yes, my mother said he was the father of our country.

Teacher: What happens when a president dies?
Student: He gets his picture on a stamp.

Teacher: Everything I say to you seems to go in one ear and out the other!
Student: Isn't that why I have two ears?

Teacher: What can you find on farms that are dangerous and have horns?
Student: Cars!

Teacher: What can birds do that people can't?
Student: Sit on telephone wires.

Student: If my teacher doesn't take back what
she said to me, I'm not ever going back to
school!
Mother: What did your teacher say that's so
terrible?
Student: She said, "You're expelled."

Teacher: Give me an example of a collective
noun.
Student: Garbage truck.

What did the paper say to the pencil?
"Write on!"

Voice on the phone: Johnny is sick and won't
be in school today.
Principal: Who is calling, please?
Voice on the phone: This is my father.

Teacher: Your spelling is terrible. You need to
buy a dictionary.
Student: I'm waiting until it comes out on video.

70

Mother: Inflation is terrible! Milk has gone up, so has bread. I wish something would go down for a change.

Student: This might be a good time to show you my report card.

Teacher: Name five things that contain milk.

Student: Ice cream, cheese, butter, a cow, and a goat.

Teacher: Why are you late for school every morning?

Student: Well, I get to the corner and then I see this sign that says, "School, Slow Down."

Teacher: What happened to your test paper?

Student: I made it into a paper airplane.

Teacher: Where did the airplane go?

Student: It got hijacked.

Teacher: If your mother earns $20 an hour and works 40 hours each week, what will she get in a year?

Student: Hopefully a new car!

Teacher: Who were the pilgrims?
Student: They were a musical group.
Teacher: Where did you get that idea?
Student: From my textbook. It says a band of
pilgrims came over on the Mayflower.

Mother: Do you hate school?
Student: No, but I hate the principal of it.

Teacher: Can you spell mouse?
Student: Yes. M–O–U–S.
Teacher: What's at the end of it?
Student: A tail.

First student: You should be a skindiver.
Second student: Why?
First student: Your grades are all at C-level.

Teacher: In which battle did Custer's last stand take place?
Student: His last one.

Why did the student glue his textbook to his head?
He thought it would make the information stick.

Mother: What could be worse than being at the bottom of a class of 20 students?
Student: Being at the bottom of a class of 30 students.

Teacher: Why was George Washington buried at Mount Vernon?
Student: He died.

What did the handsome janitor do to the pretty young teacher?
He swept her off her feet.

Teacher: Can you divide 10 apples among three people evenly?
Student: Yes. Make apple sauce.

Teacher: How do you spell hippopotamus?
Student: H–I–P–O–P–O–T–O–M–I–S.
Teacher: That isn't how it's spelled in the dictionary.
Student: I thought you asked me how *I* spelled it.

What's the difference between a fisherman and a school dropout?
A fisherman baits hooks, a dropout hates books.

Why did the computer go to the cafeteria?
To get a byte.

Student: Is it true that the law of gravity keeps
people from floating off the ground?
Teacher: Yes.
Student: What did people do before the law was
passed?

Grandfather: What is your favorite part of
school?
Rodney: Vacations.

School nurse: Do you know how you can
prevent infections from biting insects?
Student: Yes, don't bite any.

Teacher: Spell Mississippi.
Student: The river or the state?

Why was the bell expelled?
   He was a dumbbell.

Student: Mom, I saved you some money.
Mother: How did you do that?
Student: Well, you don't have to buy new
      books for me next year because I'm taking
      the same classes over.

What has 18 legs and catches flies?
   The school baseball team.

Teacher: Name four members of the cat family.
Student: Mother, father, and two kittens.

Teacher: If the mother chicken is called the hen
      and the father chicken is called a rooster,
      what are their offspring called?
Student: Eggs.

Why did the bread try out for the school play?
   It wanted to be the leading roll. *(role)*

First student: Did you hear that our science
　　teacher dates fossils?
Second student: Why? Won't women go out
　　with him?

*Why did the one-eyed professor give up
teaching?*
　　He only had one pupil.

Teacher: If the playground is on the north side,
　　which side of the school is the parking lot
　　on?
Student: The outside.

Gym coach: Swimming is one of the best forms
　　of exercise to stay thin.
Student: Then why are whales so big?

What do smart students like to sail on?
　　Scholarships.

Nellie: I think I'm a dog.
Nurse: I see. And how long has this been going
　　on?
Nellie: Since I was a puppy.

Why did the cat get kicked out of school?
   He was a cheetah. *(cheater)*

What do you call a sick librarian?
   An ill-literate.

Child: I'm glad you named me Mike.
Father: Why?
Child: That's what all the kids in school call me.

What's a music teacher's favorite Japanese food?
   Shrimp tempo-ra.

What did the ghost teacher say at the beginning of class?
   "Class, please be sheeted."

Danny: We saw the dog star at the planetarium yesterday.
Manny: Are you Sirius?

What time is it when a pie is divided among four hungry students?
   A quarter to one.

Biology teacher: Class, how do you recognize a baby snake?
Student: By its rattle.

History teacher: Class, what American had the largest family?
Gil: George Washington, the father of our country.

What geometrical figure represents a lost parrot?
  Polygon. *(Polly gone)*

Teacher: Jenny, what happened at the Boston
    Tea Party?
Jenny: I don't know, I wasn't invited.

Teacher: Janie, if you have one dollar and you
    ask your parents for another dollar, how
    many dollars would you have?
Janie: One dollar.
Teacher: Oh, dear, you don't know your math
    very well.
Janie: You don't know my parents very well.

What school building has the most stories?
  The library.

*What kind of math problems would you take to
the gym?*
  The kind that involve reducing fractions.

Mom: Wake up, you'll be late for school. It's ten
    to eight.
Junior: Who's winning?

*What's the most contradictory sign in the school
library?*
  To speak aloud is not allowed.

80

Jake: Wow, our teacher must have eyes in the back of her head!

John: Yes, her hindsight is better than her foresight.

Teacher: I'm impressed by how fast you solved that problem on the blackboard.

Student: Chalk it up to experience.

What do you get when you cross a grapefruit with a school bus?

A grapefruit that seats 45 people.

Carrie: How long have you been playing the piano?
Teacher: Fifteen years.
Carrie: Aren't your fingers tired?

What would Snow White say if she took a photography class?
   "Someday my prints will come."

What's the most disagreeable month for military students?
   A long March.

What did George Washington's father say when he saw his son's bad report card?
   "You're going down in history, son."

Where does a music teacher shop?
   At the Chopin mall.

Where does a wood-shop teacher shop?
   At the chopping mall.

Where does a geometry teacher shop?
   At the sloping mall.

Larry: My teacher says I've got the largest room.
Mary: Really?
Larry: Yes, room for improvement.

What's the hardest thing about basketball practice?
   The pavement.

Economics teacher: What's the surest way to double your money?
Class: Fold it!

What's an honest music teacher's least favorite instrument?
   A lyre. *(liar)*

Ma: I think our son is going to be an astronaut.
Pa: Why do you say that?
Ma: I talked to his principal today and she said he's taking up space.

Kit: How did you pass that geometry test without studying?
Whit: I knew all the angles.

Annie: Let's call our school newspaper *The Watermelon.*
Fannie: Why?
Annie: Because it's red (*read*) on the inside.

Why don't wood-shop students believe in glass?
  They never saw it.

Teacher: Where is your pencil, Tommy?
Tommy: I ain't got none.
Teacher: Your grammar is incorrect. You should say, "I do not have a pencil," "You do not have a pencil," or "They do not have pencils." Understand?
Tommy: No. What happened to all the pencils?

Teacher: Class, why did Paul Revere ride his horse all the way from Boston to Lexington?
Nicky: It was too heavy to carry.

Science teacher: What does it mean when the barometer is falling?
Nan: Whoever put it up didn't do a very good job.

What did the shark teacher do when his students disobeyed?
He chewed them out.

What do you say to a stuck-up choir member who wants to sing alone?
"That's so low." *(solo)*

Why are photography students the most ambitious?
　　They are always developing.

Dora: Hey, did you hear? The teacher said we'd
　　　take the test today, rain or shine!
Lora: What's so great about that?
Dora: It's snowing.

Why is an orange like a school bell?
　　Both have peels. *(peals)*

Why is an exhausted student like a car?
　　Both are tired.

Why is lightning like an unrehearsed school orchestra?
　　It doesn't know how to conduct itself.

What's a Shakespeare teacher's favorite lunch?
　　Hamlet and cheese on rye.

What's a Shakespeare teacher's favorite fast-food sandwich?
　　A Big Macbeth.

What's a history teacher's favorite kind of music?
  Plymouth Rock.

Teacher: Who can tell me what coincidence
      means?
Billy: That's funny. I was just going to ask you
      the same question.

What did the track star say when she found a hole in her stocking?
  "I gotta run."

Why do cross-country runners prefer fast food?
  They like to eat and run.

Chloe: People who swim the river in Paris are
      crazy.
Joey: What makes you say that?
Chloe: Because they're insane. *(in Seine)*

Candy: Did you hear the joke about the rotten
      cafeteria food?
Randy: No, tell me.
Candy: Forget it, you wouldn't swallow it.

Why was the spider such a good team outfielder?
Because it was always catching flies.

Did you hear about the cross-eyed teacher?
He had no control over his pupils.

Sadie: What do you think of artificial intelligence?
Katie: I'd rather have the real thing.

Why did Irving's mother knit him three stockings while he was in boarding school?
He wrote her that he had gotten so tall he had grown another foot.

Why did the skinny student avoid the letter C?
Because it makes fat a fact.

What happened to the smart hot dog?
It got on the honor roll.

Teacher: Why does the Statue of Liberty stand in New York Harbor?
Student: Because it can't sit down.

What do you call the head of a school for dinosaurs?
    The Dean-osaur.

Teacher: Louie, what comes after the letter G?
Louie: Whiz.
Teacher: And what comes after the letter T?
Louie: "V."

Why did the lazy student study his textbook only in the fall?
    Because fall turns the leaves for him.

Why did the debate teacher look to one side and then the other when he entered the classroom?
Because he couldn't see both sides at once.

Bonnie: I'm studying ancient history.
Connie: So am I. Let's get together and talk over old times.

What do a dog with a lame leg and a student adding six and seven have in common?
Both put down three and carry one.

Lizzie: My gym teacher told me to exercise with dumbbells.
Izzy: So?
Lizzie: Will you come with me to the gym?

When is a student most likely to enter a classroom?
When the door is open.

Teacher: Class, who can tell me what was the greatest feat of strength ever performed in the United States?
Student: Wheeling, West Virginia.

Why did the principal wear a big hat?
   To cover her head.

What's the most popular foot at school?
   Football games.

Which of the four seasons would you find in the school library?
   Autumn, because the leaves are turned and red. *(read)*

How do you spell elevator?
   L–F–8–R.

What happened when the science teacher mixed poison ivy and a four-leaf clover?
   She had a rash of good luck.

Teacher: Spell Tennessee.
Student: One-a-see, two-a-see, three-a-see . . .

What teachers are always unlucky?
   Miss Fortune and Miss Hap.

What teacher is hard to figure out?
   Mister E. *(mystery)*

91

Biff: Why are you the teacher's pet?
Cliff: She couldn't afford a dog.

What letter can travel the farthest?
　　The letter D, because it goes to the end of the world.

Teacher: Jimmy, name two pronouns.
Jimmy: Who, me?
Teacher: That's right.

Teacher: Do you know the meaning of fear?
Ellie: No, I'm afraid to ask.

Why is a snobby private school like a flower garden?
　　Because it's a place of haughty culture. *(horticulture)*

Why did the proud teacher display the "A +" essay on the flagpole?
　　She wanted to set an exam-pole. *(example)*

School bus driver: Is my turn signal on?
Student: Yes, no, yes, no, yes, no . . .

Why did the school librarian throw the clock out?

It tocked too much.

Father: What did you learn in school today?
Jeff: Not enough. I have to go back tomorrow.

Why was the school rich?
   There was a large diamond in its baseball field.

Ric: That bully called me an insect.
Vic: Well, he's wrong. An insect has six legs.

Librarian: Shh! The students next to you can't read.
Jack: That's too bad. I've been reading for years.

Carly: I saw a counterfeit bill in front of school today, but I walked by without picking it up.
Harley: You could be arrested!
Carly: Why?
Harley: You passed counterfeit money.

Student: Why does it rain?
Teacher: To make things grow.
Student: Then why does it rain on the sidewalk?

Why was the student hungry?
   She was ready to devour her books.

Toni: Why don't you take the bus home?
Joni: Because my parents would make me give
it back.

*Why did the pencil win the race against the
paper?*
Because the paper remained stationary.
(stationery)

Eye doctor: With these new glasses, Casey,
you'll be able to read everything!
Casey: You mean I won't have to go to school
anymore?

Art teacher: What are you drawing?
Student: A picture of a martian.
Art teacher: But no one knows what a martian
looks like.
Student: Now they will.

What's a band teacher's favorite vegetable?
Beets. *(beats)*

When is a rope like a student?
When it is taut. *(taught)*

Missy: Did you know you can eat dirt-cheap in the school cafeteria?
Cissy: Who wants to eat dirt?

First computer: Where did Mac 'n' Tosh go?
Second computer: They went data way!

Mother: Why are you taking your ruler to bed with you?
Mary Jo: To see how long I sleep.

How do you spell prisoner?
   N–J–L.

Willy: I've been seeing spots all week.
Nurse: Have you seen a doctor?
Willy: No, just spots.

What's a history teacher's favorite fruit?
   Dates.

Grandfather: Are you good at math, Sally?
Sally: Yes and no.
Grandfather: What do you mean?
Sally: Yes, I am no good at math.

Science teacher: How can you tell a dogwood
        tree from an oak tree?
Student: By its bark.

Harry: Is this my bus?
Bus driver: No, it belongs to the school.

History teacher: Class, why did the Stamp Act
        get repealed after one year?
Sally: Because the colonists licked it.

Why was the chicken kicked out of school?
    It used fowl language.

What's a baseball player's favorite anthem?
  "The Star-Spangled Batter."

Grandmother: Mikey, do you like school?
Mikey: No.
Grandmother: Why not?
Mikey: I can't read or write, and they won't let
    me talk!

Sue: How do you do so well on your tests?
Lou: I take smart pills. Want to buy some?
    They're 10 cents each.
Sue: Okay. Hey! These are just candy!
Lou: See, you're getting smarter already.

Teacher: George, what were the major turning
    points during the Revolutionary War?
George: Street corners.

Lindy: I'm really nervous about the exam today.
    I've got a headache and butterflies in my
    stomach.
Cindy: Why don't you take a couple of aspirin?
Lindy: I did, and the butterflies started playing
    tennis with them!

98

Claude: I didn't know the British Empire was sold for such a small amount.

Maude: What makes you say that?

Claude: King Richard offered his kingdom for a horse.

Teacher: How old were you on your last birthday?

Andy: Nine.

Teacher: And how old will you be on your next birthday?

Andy: Eleven.

Teacher: That's not possible.

Andy: Yes it is. Today's my tenth birthday.

Which nation do students fear most?
   Exami-nation.

Teacher: Name five animals that live in Africa.

Student: An elephant, a lion, a giraffe, and . . . two zebras.

Why is a person with her eyes closed like a bad teacher?
   She keeps her pupils in darkness.

99

What do you call the smartest duck in school?
  A wise quacker.

Teacher: You're my poorest student, yet you're
        so eager to get to my class on time. Why is
        that?
Student: I hate to miss out on any of my nap
        time.

Teacher: Can you think of a word that contains
        all the vowels?
Student: Unquestionably!

*What city is most likely found in the school
library?*
  Reading, Pennsylvania.

*What do a ringing school bell and the
Homecoming Queen have in common?*
  They're both a-pealing.

Teacher: What happened when Benjamin
        Franklin took his kite out in a
        thunderstorm?
Johnny: He was in for quite a shock.

How does the soprano in the school choir resemble a malt-shop worker?
  Both give out high screams. *(ice creams)*

Who is a photography teacher's favorite hero?
  Flash Gordon.

Auntie: Susie, what's your favorite course in school?
Susie: Lunch, because it has a first course, a second course . . .

What did one geometry theorem say to the other?
  "I'm better than you, and I have the proof."

What do you do if your dog is chewing up your textbook?
  Take the words right out of its mouth.

What game do monster schoolchildren love?
  Hide-and-Shriek.

When is a teacher not a teacher?
  When she's a bed. *(abed)*

101

Vicky: Somebody stole the fruit out of my lunch
    bag today!
Ricky: Well, that's really the pits.

Teacher: Mr. Jones from the zoo has brought a
    ten-foot snake to class today.
Daisy: You can't fool me. Snakes don't have
    feet.

Teacher: Mary, what comes after the letter A?
Mary: The rest of the alphabet.

Student: Hey, this bread is full of holes!
Cafeteria worker: What did you expect? It's
    whole wheat. *(hole)*

Student: Nurse, I feel like a dog.
Nurse: You'll be fine, but please get off the
    couch.

What has feathers and writes?
    A ballpoint hen.

Frank: What's wrong with your math teacher?
Hank: I don't know. I think she has too many
    problems to solve.

What did the music teacher say after conducting a long concert?
   "Oh, my aching Bach!"

Holly: Did you hear the joke about the eraser?
Molly: No.
Holly: Never mind, it'd rub you the wrong way.

What's brown and lives in a tower?
   The lunch bag of Notre Dame.

What has a spine but no bones and a jacket but no tie?

A textbook.

Why can't elephants go to school?

Because they can't get through the classroom door.

Benny: Did you hear the joke about the seven-foot student?
Denny: No, I didn't.
Benny: Well, it's way over your head.

Bart: Coach, I have a weak back.
Coach: When did you first notice it?
Bart: Oh, about a week back.

Lucy: Did you hear about the miser who went to the school football game?
Lacey: No, what happened?
Lucy: He thought a quarterback was a refund.

Biff: I can't be your quarterback, Coach.
Coach: Why not?
Biff: Because my mother raised me not to pass anything before saying "please!"

Biology teacher: Class, is there anything smaller
    than an ant's mouth?
Student: What the ant eats.

*How does a baseball player resemble a music
student?*
    They both play bass. *(base)*

*What's a playground supervisor's favorite kind
of music?*
    Swing.

*Why didn't the music teacher stay the whole
school year?*
    He was only a tempo-rary substitute.

*What did one lovestruck locker say to the other
locker?*
    "I think we've got the right combination."

First parent: The school choir put on a moving
    performance.
Second parent: Do you mean it was so
    wonderful it moved you to tears?
First parent: No, it moved me to the nearest
    exit.

Why didn't the students like their science teacher?
There was no chemistry between them.

Why was Benjamin Franklin so happy after he harnessed electricity?
Because then he could operate his electric shaver.

Student: I swallowed a roll of film.
Nurse: That's all right, nothing serious will develop.

How are a builder and a school-newspaper reporter alike?
Neither can create stories without foundations.

How are the letter O and a well-behaved class alike?
Both are always in order.

Why is a yardstick unusual?
It has no head or tail, but it has a foot at each end and another foot in the middle.

What pets are allowed in music class?
   Trum-pets.

Teacher: Why do you always come to school in
   wrinkled clothes?
Student: Because my mother is always mad at
   me and she won't press my clothes. What
   should I do?
Teacher: I think you and your mother should
   get things ironed out.

Science teacher: What is an atom?
Student: The guy who used to date Eve.

Knock, knock!
Who's there?
Ima.
Ima who?
Ima late for school, so quit bothering me!

Patty: I don't like vegetables. Why do they
always serve so many in the cafeteria?
Matty: Beets me.

Buffy: Teacher, can I have a dollar to give to the
man crying outside school?
Teacher: What is he crying about?
Buffy: He's crying "Ice cream, one dollar!"

Teacher: If you have three candy bars and I ask
you to give me one, how many will you
have left?
Student: Three.

Teacher: Who can tell me one thing that you
share with your parents?
Student: My homework.

Teacher: What do we call a horse doctor?
Student: A doctor with laryngitis.

108

Amy: Did you hear the joke about the jump rope?

Mike: No.

Amy: Ah, skip it.

Teacher: What one letter separates the continents of the world?

Student: C. *(sea)*

How do gymnasts solve difficult problems? They get on trampolines and jump to conclusions.

First student: When I get out of school, I'm going into the laundry business.

Second student: I think you'd be pressing your luck.

First student: What do you think about the new diving coach?

Second student: I think he's in over his head.

First student: When I grow up, I'm going to be a foot doctor.

Second student: I hope you're prepared to face defeat. *(the feet)*

109

How many books can you put into an empty desk?

One—after that it isn't empty.

Teacher: What do you want to be when you grow up?
Student: A hairdresser.
Teacher: Why?
Student: Because my mother says it's best to look for permanent work.

Mother: How are things in home economics class?
Student: Sew-sew. *(so-so)*

Teacher: Can you name one thing made long ago that is still being made today?
Student: My bed.

Teacher: How would you divide three candy bars between you and your brother?
Student: My little brother or my big brother?

Teacher: What do giraffes have that no other animals have?
Student: Baby giraffes.

Why was the elephant afraid of the computer?
  Because the computer had a mouse.

Teacher: If we breathe oxygen during the day,
    what do we breathe at night?
Student: Nitrogen.

Teacher: Why did you miss school last week?
Student: I got bit by a dog.
Teacher: Was it a rabid dog?
Student: No, it was a bird dog.

First student: Did you fill in the blank yet?
Second student: Which blank?
First student: The one between your ears.

111

First student: Last night, I fell in love with a girl at first sight.

Second student: Really, are you taking her to the prom?

First student: No, I took a second look.

First cheerleader: Whenever I'm in the dumps I go shopping for clothes.

Second cheerleader: So that's where you get them!

Teacher: Are you an avid reader?

Student: No, I've never read *Avid*.

Student: Is being a telephone operator considered a profession?

Teacher: No, it's a calling.

Kindergartner: Did Humpty Dumpty die when he fell off the wall?

Teacher: No, but now he's only a shell of a man.

Teacher: Is it possible for people to talk with fish?

Student: Yes, just drop them a line.

Kindergartner: Did you know that some dogs wear clothes?

Teacher: Who told you that?

Kindergartner: My daddy. He said in the summer a dog has a coat and pants.

Teacher: How many sides does a circle have?

Student: Two. An inside and an outside.

Teacher: Does anyone know why bears sleep all winter?

Student: Because no one is brave enough to wake them up.

Teacher: From which direction does the sun rise?

Student: Give me a minute. The answer is about to dawn on me.

First student: Did you hear the story about the pencil with erasers on both ends?

Second student: No, but it sounds pointless.

Teacher: Where's your pocket calculator?

Student: I don't need one. I already know how many pockets I have.

When do you have to drop out to graduate?
  When you're in skydiving school.

Student: Mom, should I become an electrician?
Mother: No, dear, you'll be wiring for money all
    the time.

Tiff: I want to be a seismologist.
Tal: Sounds like a pretty shaky profession to
    me.

Jody: I want to be a veterinarian.
Rodney: You'll just go to the dogs.

Student: Is it difficult to become a professional
    puppeteer?
Teacher: Well, you'll have to pull a lot of strings.

Student: How many successful landings does a
    pilot have to make before he graduates
    from flight school?
Teacher: All of them.

Teacher: Who invented spaghetti?
Student: Someone who really knew how to use
    his noodle.

114

Steve: Do you have to go to school to become a
     garbage collector?
Jane: No, you can just pick it up as you go
     along.

Tom: Do you want to hear a joke about
     bowling?
Mike: Spare me!

Lori: Where can I find a good book about trees?
Jimmy: Try a branch library.

Figure skating teacher: Why won't you get out
     on the ice?
Student: I'm afraid someone might laugh at me
     if I fall.
Figure skating teacher: No one will laugh at you,
     but the ice might make a few cracks.

Teacher: Why are you eating your lunch on the
     sidewalk?
Student: My mother said I should try to curb my
     appetite.

Which person has the most patience in school?
   The school nurse. *(patients)*

115

What did the one boy book say to the other boy book when a cute girl book walked by?
   "Check it out!"

Student: How long did it take to invent the
      rubber band?
Teacher: I believe it was done in a snap.

Kate: Do kings write their own letters?
Pete: No, they dictate.

What did the mother firefly ask the teacher?
   "Is my son bright?"

Teacher: Give me a ten-letter word that begins
      with G–A–S.
Student: Automobile.

Teacher: Can anyone tell me about Minehaha?
Student: Yes, it's a small joke.

Teacher: Where is the Red Sea?
Student: At the top of my test paper!

Student 1: What are teachers constantly
    overlooking?
Student 2: Their noses!

*What did the math book say to the
psychologist?*
    "I have problems."

How do pigs do their homework?
    With a pigpen.

*Why do school bells set a good example for
students?*
    They never speak without being tolled.

Teacher: Why are you writing that letter so
    slowly?
Student: The person I'm writing to can't read
    very fast.

117

Teacher: Why did George Washington cut
     down a cherry tree?
Student: Hmm. You got me stumped!

Teacher: Why are you crying? Are you
     homesick?
Kindergartner: No, I'm here sick.

How do you spell foe?
  N–M–E.

Teacher: Can you use the word "beans" in a
     sentence?
Student: We are all human beans.

Emily: Why did you leave school?
Amy: Illness. The teacher got sick of me.

Home economics teacher: Name three things
     that start with M and are needed to make a
     cake.
Student: Milk, margarine, and mother.

Home economics teacher: How can you keep
     milk from getting sour?
Student: Keep it in the cow.

What is the first thing you put into school each day?
   Your foot.

Accounting student: Will you help me with my
      income tax?
Teacher: Certainly.
Accounting student: Good, you know where to
      send the check.

Shawn: When should you use a soft pencil?
Honey: When you're writing love letters.

Timothy: When should you use a hard pencil?
Kimberly: When you've got a stiff exam.

Pat: Who gave you that black eye?
Pete: My girlfriend.
Pat: I thought she was out of town.
Pete: So did I.

Cafeteria cook: Have you finished filling those
      salt shakers yet?
Student worker: No, it takes a long time to put
      each piece through those little holes.

Robby: I just swallowed a whole pen full of ink.
Ricky: Incredible!
Robby: No, it was indelible.

Student: I was born in China.
Teacher: Really? What part?
Student: All of me, of course!

Music teacher: Where's Johnny?
Student: At the piano playing his half of the
    duet. I finished early.

Student: In a couple of years you'll have to look
    up to me.
Teacher: Why is that?
Student: I'm going to be a pilot.

Why is a teacher the opposite of a train?
    One says "Choo, choo," and the other says
    "Spit out the gum!"

Teacher: How did you break your leg?
Student: Well, see those steps over there?
Teacher: Yes.
Student: I didn't.

Music teacher: Do you know what a metronome
   is?
Student: Yes, it's an elf that lives in the subway.

Robert: I want to become a fisherman.
Marge: Well, I hope it doesn't make you selfish.
   (sell fish)

Teacher: Can you define nonsense?
Student: Yes, my mother says nonsense is when
   I claim my baby brother hit me.

Geography teacher: What is one difference
   between the earth and the sea?
Student: One is dirty, and the other is tide-y.

Teacher: What is the first thing that comes to
   your mind when I mention France?
Student: French fries!

*What did the spelling teacher say when she had
to borrow a dollar?*
   I–O–U–1.

Teacher: What is one of the greatest labor-
   saving inventions of today?
Student: Tomorrow.

What do you call a student who misses school?
   Homesick.

122

Spanish teacher: Did you have any trouble with your Spanish while you were in Mexico?
Student: No, but the Mexicans did.

Why did the teacher want to cross the road?
The class is always cleaner on the other side.

What happens on a clear day in southern California?
UCLA. *(You see L.A.)*

Suzy: I'm not going back to school.
Dad: Why not?
Suzy: Yesterday the teacher said that four and four make eight. Then she said that five and three make eight. Then she said that six and two make eight. I'm not going back until she makes up her mind.

Mother: Why did you swallow the money I gave you?
Child: You said it was my lunch money.

School nurse: How would you like to take your cough syrup today?
Student: With a fork.

123

Why is the letter D like a student with bad grades?
    It makes ma mad.

Why is the letter T like a lead actress at the beginning of a school play?
    It makes a star start.

Why didn't the bus get to school?
    It couldn't make the grade.

Why is a Model-T Ford like a classroom?
    It has a lot of little nuts with a crank up front.

First student: I hope I don't get a "B" on my
        report card.
Second student: Why?
First student: Don't you know that bees sting?

Principal: Please don't tell anyone the salary
        we've offered you.
New teacher: Don't worry. I'm just as
        embarrassed about it as you are.

124

What's worse than raining cats and dogs?
Hailing school buses.

Student: Teacher, my computer is getting old.
Teacher: Really?
Student: I think it has a loss of memory.

What does a geography teacher use when she hosts a dinner party?
China.

Science teacher: Class, your microscopes
    magnify three times.
Student: Oh, no! I've already used it twice!

Teacher: You've made a lot of spelling errors.
    Whenever you're in doubt, look the word
    up in the dictionary.
Student: What if you're never in doubt?